W9-CKI-651

The Dreamers and DACA

Other titles in the *Immigration Issues* series include:
Birthright Citizenship
Border Control and the Wall
Detaining and Deporting Undocumented Immigrants
Refugees and Asylum

Immigration
ISSUES

The Dreamers and DACA

Barbara Sheen

DUBUQUE COUNTY LIBRARY

ReferencePoint
Press

San Diego, CA

© 2020 ReferencePoint Press, Inc.
Printed in the United States

For more information, contact:
ReferencePoint Press, Inc.
PO Box 27779
San Diego, CA 92198
www.ReferencePointPress.com

ALL RIGHTS RESERVED.
No part of this work covered by the copyright hereon may be reproduced or used in any form or by any means—graphic, electronic, or mechanical, including photocopying, recording, taping, web distribution, or information storage retrieval systems—without the written permission of the publisher.

LIBRARY OF CONGRESS CATALOGING-IN-PUBLICATION DATA

Names: Sheen, Barbara, author.
Title: The Dreamers and DACA/By Barbara Sheen.
Description: San Diego, CA: ReferencePoint Press, Inc., [2020] | Series:
  Immigration Issues | Includes bibliographical references and index. |
  Audience: Grades 10–12
Identifiers: LCCN 2019034572 (print) | LCCN 2019034573 (ebook) | ISBN
  9781682827697 (library binding) | ISBN 9781682827703 (ebook)
Subjects: LCSH: Illegal alien children—United States—Juvenile literature.
  | Deportation—United States—Juvenile literature. | Adult children of
  immigrants—United States—Juvenile literature. | Emigration and
  immigration law—United States—Juvenile literature.
Classification: LCC JV6600 .S54 2020 (print) | LCC JV6600 (ebook) | DDC
  362.7086/9120973—dc23
LC record available at https://lccn.loc.gov/2019034572
LC ebook record available at https://lccn.loc.gov/2019034573

Contents

American in All Ways but One

Luis is a young software engineer who was brought to the United States from Mexico seventeen years ago by his parents when he was in the second grade. At the time, he had no understanding of the concept of borders or immigration laws or any control over his parents' decision to slip into the United States without proper authorization. "I didn't know what it all meant,"[1] he explains.

The family settled in California, where Luis attended public school. He quickly learned to speak English, made friends, and grew up much like his American-born peers, celebrating the same holidays, watching the same movies, and playing on the same sports teams. He felt like an American, but because he is an undocumented immigrant, he faced obstacles that most teens never experience. Without legal status or a Social Security number, he could not legally work, travel by air, qualify for in-state tuition at a state college, obtain student financial aid, or get a driver's license, among other things. He explains:

At that time, in California, you couldn't have a driver's license if you didn't have a social security number. . . . When we started looking into financial aid, they as well ask you for a social security number. Again, I noticed that I was never going to get the same opportunities as others; especially in high school when students are at that age when they can start applying for driving permits or jobs during the summer.[2]

Luis had spent most of his life in California. He felt no ties—emotional or otherwise—to Mexico. Yet under immigration law he was considered a lawbreaker and faced the threat of deportation.

Luis's future seemed bleak. For as long as he can remember, he dreamed of a career in computer science, which requires a college degree. In an effort to make his dream come true, he worked very hard in high school, took advanced placement and honors classes, and participated in extracurricular activities. But without the benefit of in-state tuition or financial aid, he could not afford college. Nor could he legally work without a Social Security number. "I felt terrible," he says. "I think that's one of the saddest parts of being [undocumented]."[3]

Dreamers and DACA

The establishment of the Deferred Action for Childhood Arrivals (DACA) program helped Luis achieve his goals. Enacted by executive order in 2012 by President Barack Obama, it was created to shield eligible undocumented young people from the threat of

People protest the Trump administration's immigration policies. Up to 1.9 million undocumented immigrants were brought to the United States as minors. They are known as Dreamers.

deportation for a two-year renewable period. It also allows them to obtain a Social Security number and a driver's license, work legally, and qualify for in-state college tuition in their state of residence. It does not, however, offer participants a path to citizenship.

Since the program began, about 800,000 individuals have been given DACA status. They are part of an estimated 1.1 million to 1.9 million undocumented immigrants who were brought to the United States as minors. As a group, these young people are known as Dreamers. The name comes from the Development, Relief, and Education for Alien Minors Act, or Dream Act, a legislative proposal first introduced in 2001 that would have given Dreamers much the same protection as DACA plus a path to citizenship. However, the original bill and subsequent versions were never passed by Congress.

In response to Congress's inability to pass a 2011 version of the Dream Act, Obama established DACA as a temporary way to help and protect eligible Dreamers until permanent legislation could be enacted. Although most Dreamers are potentially eligible for DACA status, not all applied for the program during the time when new applications were being accepted. Some could not afford the cost of applying, and others did not meet all the requirements. Other Dreamers feared that submitting personal data to the federal government could backfire, and the information could be used to locate and deport them or members of their family.

An Uncertain Future

Despite the help DACA has given Dreamers, some Americans believe it is unconstitutional. They base this view on the fact that the program was established by executive order rather than through legislative action. In 2017 the Trump administration moved to rescind DACA. Various legal challenges and appeals have been moving through the courts. Preliminary rulings have kept the program open and allowed current DACA recipients to renew their status, but no new applications were being accepted. In June 2019 the Supreme Court announced it would hear the case in its next term, which was scheduled to begin in October 2019. A ruling was not expected until 2020. A ruling in favor of terminating the program would put all Dreamers, including DACA recipients, at risk of being uprooted from their current lives and sent back to countries that they barely know. However, if Congress wanted to protect this population, it could still pass the Dream Act or a similar law.

Reflecting on the possibility of being forced to leave the only country he has known, Everardo Chavez, a DACA recipient, says, "That's something I never want to think about. . . . We've pretty much grown up here all our life loving this country and everything and, you know, saluting the flag, saying the pledge of allegiance all of my life. I don't know the pledge of allegiance for Mexico because I didn't grow up there. I feel like I am American."[4]

"We've pretty much grown up here all our life loving this country . . . saluting the flag, saying the pledge of allegiance. . . . I feel like I am American."[4]

—Everardo Chavez, DACA recipient

Chapter One

Changing Policies

Changing attitudes toward
immigration in general—and
illegal immigration in particular—
and government policies that reflect
those changing attitudes lie at the heart
of the plight of the young people known as
Dreamers. History and politics play a significant
role in influencing these attitudes and policies.

History and the Dreamers

Until the late nineteenth century, the United States had almost
no immigration controls. The borders were unsecured. Visas and
passports were not required to enter the country, and the concept of illegal immigration did not exist. However, during the late
nineteenth and early twentieth centuries, as more and more immigrants from southern and eastern Europe and China flooded
into the United States, many Americans became resentful and
distrustful of the new arrivals. They influenced lawmakers to enact policies and set up agencies to control and limit immigration.
Additional policies followed in the twentieth century. Depending
on politics and public attitudes at the time, some of these policies favored immigration, while others added new restrictions.
Restrictive laws passed in 1921 and 1924, for instance, capped
the number of immigrants allowed into the country each year
and imposed numerical quotas based on nationality. The quotas
favored immigrants from northern and western Europe. But a
1965 law replaced nationality-based quotas with a system that
favored family reunification and immigrants with certain skills.
This law opened up immigration to more people from Asia and

Latin America. Other laws, particularly those enacted in the 1980s and 1990s, further liberalized immigration policies, especially for refugees and undocumented immigrants.

After foreign terrorists attacked the United States on September 11, 2001, public attitudes toward immigrants (legal and unauthorized) hardened. The hijackers were neither immigrants nor undocumented; all had entered the country on temporary visas. Nevertheless, Americans felt vulnerable and suspicious of

Clouds of smoke billow from the World Trade Center towers in New York City during the September 11, 2001, terrorist attacks. Afterward, public attitudes hardened toward immigrants, especially those from largely Muslim countries.

foreigners. As a result, immigration and border security became a national security issue. In an effort to keep dangerous people out of the country, more restrictions, including stepped-up border security, were put in place, and the US Immigration and Customs Enforcement (ICE) was established. ICE's primary mission is the enforcement of immigration laws, which includes identifying, locating, detaining, and removing unauthorized immigrants.

As increasingly stringent immigration policies were enacted, it became more difficult for people to get authorization to enter the United States legally or, for those who did enter legally, to renew expired visas. Faced with these obstacles, many immigrant families entered the country illegally or overstayed the terms of their visas. Many of the children in these families would eventually become known as "Dreamers," a label that was given to them after the original Dream Act was introduced in 2001.

The Dream Act

The original version of the Dream Act was introduced in Congress shortly before the 9/11 terrorist attacks. Even before the attacks, distrust of undocumented immigrants was increasing. However, some lawmakers did not view the group who would become known as the Dreamers as a threat. In addition, many thought that deporting these young people, most of whom had received a free public education in the United States, did not make sense economically. As sociologist and author William A. Schwab, explains, "The bottom line is we are wasting our nation's investment in these children."[5]

Some Americans also felt that it was unfair to hold these young people accountable for their parents' actions. As Colorado senator Cory Gardner explained,

"The bottom line is we are wasting our nation's investment in these children."[5]

—William A. Schwab, sociologist and author

What a Dream Act Would Do

A number of different versions of the Dream Act have been proposed over the years. Although these have had some key differences, they all would have provided Dreamers a path to citizenship. However, gaining citizenship is not immediate or guaranteed. Under the Dream Act, individuals who were brought to the United States as minors, who have not been convicted of a crime, and meet specific age, residency, and education requirements are eligible to obtain conditional permanent residency status. This allows them to live, work, and study in the United States for a period of ten years.

During this ten-year period, individuals who have completed at least two years of higher education or a program leading to professional certification or licensing, or two years of military service, can obtain lawful permanent residency status, also known as green card status. This allows them to permanently live, work, and study in the United States, among other benefits.

After five years, green card holders can apply for US citizenship. To be granted citizenship, eligible applicants must be able to speak, read, and write English and must successfully complete a civics exam. The exam tests an individual's knowledge of US history and government. Individuals who meet all the requirements are granted naturalized citizenship, which gives them all the rights of citizens born in the United States.

"Their parents made a decision to enter this country illegally. . . . They [the children] deserve to be afforded some form of legal status that recognizes that they are here through no fault of their own. . . . This is an issue of fairness, decency, and compassion."[6]

With these reasons in mind, lawmakers proposed the Development, Relief, and Education for Alien Minors Act, or Dream Act. The original act, and subsequent variations, would have allowed qualified undocumented immigrants who were brought to the United States as children to legally live and work in the United States without threat of deportation, as well as providing them with a path to citizenship.

> "Their parents made a decision to enter this country illegally. . . . They [the children] deserve to be afforded some form of legal status that recognizes that they are here through no fault of their own."[6]
>
> —Cory Gardner, former US senator

The act also made these young people eligible for in-state tuition in public colleges in the states in which they resided. To gain these benefits, individuals had to meet certain requirements, which varied somewhat depending on the version of the bill. In the original version of the Dream Act, these requirements included being between ages twelve and thirty-five at the time of application, having entered the United States before age sixteen, continuously residing in the country for five consecutive years prior to the bill's enactment, having successfully completed high school or the equivalent, having been accepted in an institute of higher education or having served or been accepted to serve in the US military for a minimum of two years, and being of good moral character.

Not all Americans or all lawmakers supported the bill. Some conservative Republicans, in particular, thought that the act undermined existing immigration laws by granting amnesty to people who had entered the country illegally. They also maintained that by protecting Dreamers, the act unfairly rewarded these young people's parents, who had knowingly broken immigration laws. And opponents of the act worried that it would encourage other undocumented foreigners to bring their children to the United States. For these and other reasons, Congress did not pass the 2001 Dream Act. In the following eighteen years, at least ten versions of the Dream Act were proposed as freestanding bills or as amendments to other bills, but they too were rejected.

DACA

Over the years, the Dreamers pinned their hopes for a stable future on the passage of a Dream Act. Each time it failed, they faced renewed frustration. As Tam Tran, a Dreamer, told members of Congress in 2007, "Without the Dream Act, I will have no chance of getting out of the immigration limbo I'm in. I will always be a perpetual foreigner in a country I've always felt I belonged in."[7]

"Without the Dream Act, I will have no chance of getting out of the immigration limbo I'm in. I will always be a perpetual foreigner in a country I've always felt I belonged in."[7]

—Tam Tran, Dreamer

A young male immigrant from Honduras is assisted with applying for DACA status, which would prevent him from being deported. Thousands of Dreamers applied for DACA status before the program was closed to new applicants.

Although deportations of unauthorized immigrants increased significantly during the Obama administration, the focus was on deporting individuals who had committed felony crimes, rather than law-abiding undocumented individuals. Indeed, Obama supported protecting the Dreamers. Influenced by young Dreamer activists and their supporters and frustrated by Congress's failure to enact yet another version of the Dream Act, on June 15, 2012, Obama signed an executive order establishing the Deferred Action for Childhood Arrivals program, or DACA. It was, according to author and journalist Laura Wides-Muñoz, "the most dramatic immigration reform program the United States had seen in nearly three decades."[8] Nevertheless, its establishment angered those lawmakers and Americans who were opposed to helping unauthorized immigrants.

DACA was created as a temporary measure until permanent legislation could be enacted. Under DACA, qualified Dreamers are classified as "lawfully present" in the United States. This classification allows them to live in the United States for a two-year

President Obama Announces the Establishment of DACA

President Barack Obama signed an executive order establishing DACA on June 15, 2012. Below is an excerpt from the speech he made announcing the program. He described this action as an effort

> to mend our nation's immigration policy, to make it more fair, more efficient, and more just—specifically for certain young people sometimes called "Dreamers." These are young people who study in our schools, they play in our neighborhoods, they're friends with our kids, they pledge allegiance to our flag. They are Americans in their heart, in their minds, in every single way but one: on paper. They were brought to this country by their parents—sometimes even as infants—and often have no idea that they're undocumented until they apply for a job or a driver's license, or a college scholarship.
>
> Put yourself in their shoes. Imagine you've done everything right your entire life—studied hard, worked hard, maybe even graduated at the top of your class—only to suddenly face the threat of deportation to a country that you know nothing about, with a language that you may not even speak. . . . It makes no sense to expel talented young people, who . . . want to staff our labs, or start new businesses, or defend our country simply because of the actions of their parents—or because of the inaction of politicians.

Quoted in White House, "Remarks by the President on Immigration," June 15, 2012. https://obama whitehouse.archives.gov.

renewable period without threat of deportation and gives them the same benefits as the Dream Act. However, it does not offer participants a path to citizenship.

In order to qualify for DACA, applicants must meet similar requirements to those of the Dream Act. DACA recipients can apply to renew their enrollment each time it expires, indefinitely. There is no age cap on renewals. Applicants are required to submit their fingerprints, provide a number of documents disclosing personal information, and pay $495 for the initial application and each renewal application.

Thousands of Dreamers immediately applied for DACA. Many of those who did not apply were under or over the age threshold. In fact, an estimated 250,000 Dreamers who currently meet the initial application requirements were too young to apply for DACA before the Trump administration closed the program to new applicants. Others did not meet residency or education requirements, or they feared that revealing personal data might put undocumented members of their family at risk of deportation. Many could not afford the application fee. But for those who did enroll, DACA proved to be transformational. As Julia, a teacher and DACA recipient, explains, "It's the single reason I am able to teach, and live on my own, and pay for my car, and feel like I belong in the country I have lived in for 15 years."[9]

Expanded DACA

In 2014, with Congress caught in political gridlock and still no passage of a Dream Act in sight, Obama once again took executive action. This action expanded DACA by removing the thirty-year upper age cap for initial application. The executive action also established the Deferred Action for Parents of Americans and Lawful Permanent Residents (DAPA) program. Similar to DACA, it would have given temporary protection from deportation to undocumented parents of children born in the United States and/or the parents of lawful permanent residents if they met certain requirements.

Under the Fourteenth Amendment of the Constitution, all babies born in the United States (except those born to foreign diplomats or other government officials from foreign countries) are American citizens, no matter their parentage. This is known as birthright citizenship. Expanded DACA/DAPA would have protected an estimated 25 percent of Dreamers who are parents of US citizens. However, shortly after Obama announced the expanded DACA/DAPA policy, a number of Republican-led states

17

sued to block its establishment. They maintained that because the new policy was created by executive order rather than legislative action, it was unconstitutional. They also argued that by expanding DACA and establishing DAPA, the president failed to enforce existing immigration laws.

A federal district court judge agreed and issued a preliminary injunction blocking the new policy. In 2015 the Obama administration appealed the case to the Supreme Court. At the time, the Supreme Court had only eight justices, due to the death of Justice Antonin Scalia, and a tie vote occurred. By law, in cases of a tie, the lower court ruling stands. Therefore, enactment of the new policy was quashed. This did not affect the existing DACA program.

Phasing Out DACA

By the 2016 presidential election, issues related to illegal immigration had become even more highly charged. In fact, the Republican candidate for president, Donald Trump, vowed that if elected he would immediately terminate DACA. He referred to the policy as illegal amnesty and declared it unconstitutional because it was established by executive order and challenged existing immigration laws. "In a Trump administration," he declared, "all immigration laws will be enforced. . . . No one will be immune or exempt from enforcement—and ICE and Border Patrol officers will be allowed to do their jobs. Anyone who has entered the United States illegally is subject to deportation."[10]

On September 5, 2017, President Trump signed an executive order phasing out DACA. Jeff Sessions, the attorney general at the time, justified the action on the grounds that DACA had "the same legal and constitutional defects that the courts recognized as to DAPA."[11] Therefore, he argued, when the Supreme Court allowed the lower court's ruling blocking the

"In a Trump administration all immigration laws will be enforced. . . . Anyone who has entered the United States illegally is subject to deportation."[10]

—Donald Trump, forty-fifth president of the United States

expanded DACA/DAPA to stand, it set a legal precedent that also applied to the original DACA.

Under Trump's plan, the DACA program was closed to new applications, but no one's DACA status would be revoked until it expired. Those enrollees whose DACA status was set to expire on or before March 5, 2018, were given a six-month window in which they could apply to renew their status for another two years. Once this window closed, no renewal applications would be accepted. The Trump administration gave Congress the same six-month period to come up with a legislative alternative to DACA. However, Congress failed to come up with a solution. So in all cases, once their status expired, DACA participants became subject to deportation.

Trump's action was praised by anti-illegal immigration advocates and condemned by groups that supported the Dreamers. It was challenged in court by fifteen Democrat-led states and a number of pro-Dreamer advocacy groups. By April 2018 a number of federal courts had issued temporary injunctions that kept DACA alive on the grounds that the rescission was based on inaccurate legal claims. The courts reasoned that since the Supreme Court's vote on expanded DACA/DAPA was a split decision, no legal precedent had been set, which made the administration's reasoning faulty. Under the court rulings, current DACA recipients can file to renew their DACA protection, but no new applicants can apply for DACA.

Unhappy with this turn of events, the Trump administration petitioned the Supreme Court to review the lower courts' rulings. Until a permanent decision is made by the Supreme Court or a Dream Act is enacted by Congress, these young people remain in limbo. As Rosa, a DACA recipient, explains, "It kind of feels like I was living in a glass house and everything broke, everything shattered."[12]

A Political Football

Although Trump rescinded DACA, at times he has also expressed sympathy for the Dreamers. By late 2018 the fate of these undocumented young people had become a political football, with supporters and opponents using the Dreamers' plight to gain political advantage. As part of his crackdown on illegal immigration, Trump vowed to build a continuous border wall across the United States' southern border. At first he said that Mexico would pay for the wall. When Mexico rejected the idea, the president turned to Congress. In December 2018 he requested that $25 billion be added to a proposed appropriations bill, which would renew funding for the government for the 2019 fiscal year. Republicans supported Trump's request, while Democrats opposed it, leading to a political standoff.

In an effort to garner support from Democratic legislators who were against funding the wall, the president tried to use the Dreamers as a bargaining chip. In exchange for funds for the wall,

Workers place sections of a barrier being erected between the United States and Mexico. President Trump vowed to build a wall that spans the entire southern US border.

he proposed a temporary extension of DACA, which would have allowed recipients to keep their protections for three more years. Democratic leaders rejected the offer because it did not provide the Dreamers with permanent protection. As US senator Richard Blumenthal said, "It's neither serious nor credible as a real remedy for Dreamers."[13]

Due to this impasse, legislators could not agree on an appropriations bill. Consequently, the federal government shut down from December 22, 2018, to January 25, 2019. The shutdown negatively affected many Americans. Faced with public pressure to end the shutdown, Congress agreed to temporarily reopen the government on January 25, 2019, while the lawmakers worked on an appropriations bill. A bill was finally passed on February 14, 2019. It provided nearly $1.4 billion dollars for the construction of a small section of a border wall but did not address the Dreamers.

This left the Dreamers in essentially the same position they were in years earlier: deeply entangled with politics, history, and changing public attitudes toward illegal immigration. As DACA recipient Humberto Marquez laments, "Sometimes I feel like it's all a . . . game."[14]

Chapter Two

Who Are the Dreamers?

Of the estimated 1.1 million to 1.9 million Dreamers currently living in the United States, about 800,000 are DACA recipients. They were brought to this country in many ways and for a variety of reasons. Some entered the United States legally on temporary visas, which they later overstayed; others entered illegally, facing hard and dangerous journeys. In many cases, once they were living in the United States, their parents tried unsuccessfully to update the family's visas or get permanent resident status. However, doing so can be very difficult.

From Countries Worldwide

Americans generally assume that all Dreamers are from Mexico—and many are. According to the US Citizenship and Immigration Services, about 78 percent of all Dreamers were born in Mexico. The remaining 22 percent come from around the globe. They come from the Philippines and the Central American nations of El Salvador, Guatemala, and Honduras. They come from countries such as Brazil, Venezuela, and Argentina in South America and from Caribbean nations including Jamaica and Dominican Republic. Dreamers have also come from countries such as Poland and Ireland in Europe and South Korea and India in Asia.

Dreamers have settled in different parts of the United States. The largest number, about 598,000, live in California. Other states with large Dreamer populations include Texas, Florida, New York, Illinois, and Arizona. Cities with large

Dreamer populations, ranging from ten thousand to more than one hundred thousand, include Los Angeles, San Francisco, San Diego, Chicago, New York City, Phoenix, Atlanta, Denver, Dallas-Fort Worth, Houston, Las Vegas, Portland, Seattle, and Washington, DC.

According to a 2017 survey conducted by Tom Wong, professor of political science at the University of California, San Diego, most Dreamers arrived in the United States when they were about six years old and are currently in their mid-twenties. Many live in mixed-status families that comprise both US citizens and unauthorized immigrants. One-fourth are parents of US citizens, and many have younger siblings who were born in the United States. Dreamers are fairly evenly divided between males and females, with the female population slightly higher at 53 percent. Many Dreamers are students; some are pursuing advanced degrees. Those who are DACA recipients tend to be better educated, be employed in higher-skilled jobs, and earn more money than other undocumented immigrants. In fact, as a group, DACA recipients earn a total of about $30 billion per year.

Freedom and Opportunity

All Dreamers are in the United States because their parents chose to come here from another country. It takes a lot of courage for people to uproot themselves and their family from their homeland and move to a country where they are often unwelcome and unfamiliar with the language, culture, and social norms. Most leave behind extended family, friends, pets, possessions, and the only life they have ever known.

Knowing the risks involved, it also requires a certain level of courage—or desperation—to slip into the United States illegally or to overstay an expired visa. So why do people do it? Most unauthorized immigrants have a similar response to that question. They say that they came to the United States seeking opportunity, freedom, and most of all, a better life for

Dulce Garcia (pictured) came to the United States as a child with her undocumented parents and put herself through college and law school to become an attorney. Many Dreamers are good students and go on to earn advanced degrees.

their children. Many faced terrible economic conditions in their country of origin. Poverty, high unemployment, unhealthy working conditions, corruption, and lack of educational opportunity can wear people down and make the future seem grim. So they leave. As Alma Aparicio, a Dreamer, explains:

My mother brought me to this country at the age of three because she wanted me to grow up and have an education so that one day, I could have the option to become a doctor and heal people, or become a lawyer and defend people, and even become an architect and build something amazing! In the eyes of my mom everything was a possibility, but cleaning people's houses, like she's been doing since she was 13, wasn't one of them. Coming to America, the land of opportunity, was the only way she thought any of this could ever happen.[15]

Others left their homeland to escape from crime, domestic or gang violence, civil unrest, armed conflict, or oppression. Some of these individuals present themselves to border patrol agents at the border, requesting legal entry as an asylum seeker. Asylum seekers are individuals looking for international protection out of fear of being hurt, killed, or persecuted in their native country. Individuals must meet stiff requirements to be granted asylum. Many potential asylum seekers fear that they will not meet these requirements. Rather than risk being sent back to a dangerous land, they enter the United States illegally or via a temporary visa, which they overstay. For example, more than twenty-eight thousand Dreamers came from El Salvador, which the United Nations considers one of the most violent nations in the world. On average, more than ten homicides occur there each day. Much of the violence is aimed at children, especially young girls. In fact, more than forty-three hundred attacks against girls ages twelve to seventeen were reported in 2018 alone. It is not surprising that these young people's parents broke immigration laws in order to keep their children safe. As Karen Perez, a teacher and DACA recipient explains: "I feel like it's common sense: If something bad is going on, you flee, right? You want a better future for your kids, and so, you bring your kids."[16]

> "I feel like it's common sense: If something bad is going on, you flee, right? You want a better future for your kids, and so, you bring your kids."[16]
>
> —Karen Perez, teacher and DACA recipient

Coming to the United States with a Visa

The Dreamers were brought to the United States in a variety of ways. Many arrived through legal ports of entry such as airports and official border crossings, where they came under the scrutiny of federal agents. These individuals held some type of temporary nonimmigrant visa, which allowed them to enter the United States legally and stay for a specific period of time. Temporary nonimmigrant visas include a variety of tourist, student, business, medical, and work visas. Visas are issued to

A Dreamer's Journey

Elvin is a Dreamer. In an article on the website Faces of DACA, he describes why he and his family left their home in Mexico and entered the United States without authorization:

> I was born in the notorious state of Sinaloa. The state at the time had a really high crime rate and an overall bad economy. It was like the wild west, but with more ruthless individuals and more advanced weapons. We ended up moving a lot across Mexico, eventually ended up in Mexico City. . . .
>
> My dad wanted something better for us and decided to bring us to the U.S. He chose Oregon since he had some cousins living there at the time, making it easier to settle. Before coming to the States, we tried everything possible to come here legally, but it was very difficult at the time. There were a lot of requirements we did not meet. My parents kept on filing the paperwork to get a visa, but kept getting rejected for over a year. My dad eventually got tired of waiting and made the decision to bring us over illegally. I was about 9 years old and had no say.

Quoted in Faces of DACA, "Elvin's Journey," September 12, 2017. www.facesofdaca.us.

a limited number of qualified individuals at a US embassy or consulate located in their country of origin. Most temporary nonimmigrant visas allow minor children to accompany their parents. The children are issued visas that have the same expiration date as those of their parents.

Not all visas are the same. The length of time visa holders can legally remain in the United States depends on the type of visa they hold. Tourist and business visas, for example, extend from a few days to six months, while medical visas may be valid for a year, and student and worker visas can span many years. No matter the type of visa, when the term of a visa expires, visa holders no longer have legal authorization to be in the United States. In order to remain in the United States legally, they must apply for an extension to stay, which is very difficult to obtain. If this is not a possibility, they are expected to leave the country. But many do not leave.

Indeed, according to a study conducted by the Center for Migration Studies, about 44 percent of all undocumented immigrants living in the United States are visa overstays. Many are Dreamers whose parents decided to remain in the country without authorization once the family's visas expired. That is what happened to Mo. He is a Dreamer who accompanied his parents to the United States from Iran so that his father could study mathematics at the University of Michigan. The student visa that allowed his father to do this expired once he earned his degree. By then economic conditions in Iran had changed for the worse. Rather than going back, the family decided to stay in the United States illegally. Mo, who was too young to understand what was happening, had no say in the matter.

Crossing the Southern Border

Other undocumented immigrants bypass the legal entry process entirely. They slip into the United States through the southern border and, less commonly, the northern border. Many Dreamers from Mexico and Central America came to the United States in this manner. Their journey to the United States was often long and perilous. In many cases it involved hiking through treacherous desert terrain in blistering heat without sufficient water, adequate food, or proper clothes. In fact, although there is no system that tracks how many migrants die trying to cross the southern border each year, the border patrol reports finding the remains of 6,915 migrants from 1998 to 2016. Indeed, it is not uncommon for Dreamers to know someone who died trying to sneak into the United States.

Once individuals arrive at the border, getting across is no easy matter. Federal agents patrol the border on foot, on horseback, and in all-terrain vehicles. Many of their vehicles are equipped with infrared cameras and ground-scanning radar devices, which can detect even small movements for about a 15-mile (24 km) radius. Immigrants must be lucky to make it across without getting caught. Many Dreamers report trying to cross with their families multiple times before actually getting through. Rosie, a DACA recipient, recalls her experience:

> Crossing the border is one of the saddest events that I remember as a child. We tried many times to cross the border, failing to do so again and again. . . . We didn't have any money. We had to sleep on the streets near the border. We were really cold and hungry because we didn't have any blankets or food. The thing I remember the most is when my sister went up to this lady—we were starving—so she went up to this lady who was selling Maruchan soups and asked her for two soups, one for me and one for her. She gave us each something to eat and that was the first time that I had one of those soups. A man who was selling serapes [blankets] saw how we were shivering, and he came over to give my mom one so we can make ourselves warm. We still have those blankets today. We were at the border for about three weeks trying to cross.[17]

In an effort to get to the United States safely, many immigrants hire smugglers to help them. For fees starting at about $4,000 per person, depending on the geographic location, smugglers lead groups of immigrants through Mexico to the US border. However, smugglers are often untrustworthy. They have been known to attack, rob, rape, and/or abandon their charges. Even when smugglers are reputable, the journey is never easy. Maria, a DACA recipient, came to the United States from Guatemala when she was thirteen. Her mother, who was living in Los Angeles as an undocumented immigrant at that time,

"Crossing the border is one of the saddest events that I remember as a child. We tried many times to cross the border, failing to do so again and again."[17]

—Rosie, DACA recipient

A customs and border patrol agent surveys the fence at the border between Arizona and Mexico. Agents patrol the border on foot, on horseback, and in all-terrain vehicles.

paid smugglers to bring her daughter to the United States. Maria had no real understanding of what she was doing. She had never left her village before, she knew nothing about immigration laws, and she had no say in the decision to enter illegally. All she knew was that she would be reunited with her mother. Author Kirk W. Johnson describes Maria's monthlong journey:

> At the border between Guatemala and Mexico, Maria joined a group of twenty people, most of them from El Salvador and Honduras. When the sun set, their smugglers pointed to a mountain path and told them to start walking. On the other side, they were loaded into a box truck in two rows. Jugs of water were passed out—one for every three people—to help passengers cope with the sweltering heat. When the truck climbed or descended hills, its cargo tumbled around, humans piling painfully onto other humans.[18]

Becoming Documented

Once established in the United States, Dreamers would not need DACA's temporary protections if they could obtain legal permanent resident status. This status allows eligible foreign-born immigrants to permanently live and work in the United States without threat of deportation. Individuals must hold legal permanent resident status for a minimum of five years before they can apply for citizenship. DACA does not grant participants legal permanent residence status, but a Dream Act would.

Currently, it is very difficult for Dreamers to change their immigration status and get legal permanent resident status. Although some Dreamers do obtain legal permanent resident status by being sponsored by an immediate family member who is either a US citizen or a legal permanent resident, there

Cracking Down on Visa Overstays

As part of his illegal immigration policy, in April 2019 Donald Trump signed a memorandum cracking down on foreigners who overstay the terms of their visas. Those to be targeted include Dreamers without DACA protections. In the memorandum, Trump wrote, "Although the United States benefits from legitimate (nonimmigrant) entry, individuals who abuse the visa process and decline to abide by the terms and conditions of their visas, including their visa departure dates, undermine the integrity of our immigration system and harm the national interest."

In the memorandum, the president ordered the secretary of state and the secretary of homeland security to come up with ways to discourage visa overstays. Suggestions included punishing nations whose citizens have high rates of visa overstays by imposing fees or tariffs on these nations and/or withholding foreign aid to those countries. Other suggestions included requiring people entering the United States on visas to pay an admission fee, which would be repaid once the visa holder leaves the country.

Quoted in Alan Gomez, "President Donald Trump Orders Crackdown on 'Visa Overstays' in Latest Push Against Illegal Immigration," *USA Today*, April 22, 2019. www.usatoday.com.

A Mexican immigrant meets with his attorney. Many Dreamers turn to immigration lawyers to help them with the complicated application process in the hope of obtaining US citizenship.

is a huge backlog of applications, leading to long delays in processing these applications. In fact, the wait time can be decades. Humberto Marquez, a Dreamer and citizenship application specialist at the Fort Smith Adult Education Center in Arkansas, explains, "People think that you get in this line, you sign some papers, and in a few months, you get a green card [a permit that indicates that the holder has legal permanent resident status]. . . . We get clients (at the Adult Education Center) who wait up to 25 or 30 years to get their green card."[19]

Not only can it take years to acquire legal status, it can be quite complicated and expensive. Many applicants turn to an immigration lawyer to guide them through the application process. However, immigration law is a very complex field. It is not unusual for applicants to be taken advantage of by inept or unscrupulous lawyers. Plus, there is no guarantee that even the most competent and trustworthy lawyer will succeed. DACA recipient Leezia Dhalla explains:

"What so many don't understand is that people aren't undocumented for lack of trying. So much factors into this horrible circumstance."[20]

—Leezia Dhalla, DACA recipient

What so many don't understand is that people aren't undocumented for lack of trying. So much factors into this horrible circumstance. For 20 years, my parents have tried incredibly hard to become permanent residents. They spent tens of thousands of dollars on paperwork and legal fees, only for their applications to languish in the system. We didn't get money back when our lawyer screwed up our paperwork. . . . The process to becoming a permanent resident or citizen of this country is so drawn out and complex.[20]

Not surprisingly, like Leezia, many Dreamers are frustrated by the legalization process, which they hope will be reformed in the future.

Chapter Three

Many Challenges

Like almost all undocumented immigrants, Dreamers face many challenges in their lives. These challenges affect their physical, mental, and emotional health; their day-to-day lives; and the way they view the future. The implementation of DACA helped ease many of these burdens. But the rescission of the program and the uncertainty about what will happen next has brought back old issues and introduced new ones.

Fitting In

Beginning a new life in a foreign country is never easy. Like many other immigrants, young Dreamers face language barriers that, at least initially, put them at a disadvantage academically. They must learn English while also adjusting to a new culture and social norms. Those who live in ethnically diverse communities are often taught by teachers trained to work with speakers of other languages, which helps these learners progress academically. Some Dreamers, however, live in regions with very few of these specially trained educators. It is not unusual for these youngsters to lag behind in school. This can frustrate them, lower their self-esteem, and discourage them from completing high school or pursuing postsecondary education.

Moreover, some young Dreamers face teasing and bullying at school, which is linked to many negative outcomes, including depression, anxiety, feelings of isolation, poor school performance, and diminished self-esteem. Bullying and teasing is especially a problem for Dreamers who grow up in less diverse regions, where they are more likely to stand out from their peers. Children and adolescents are often cruel to anyone who looks, sounds, or acts different from everyone else. Like most kids, young Dreamers want to be accepted by their classmates. So in an effort to fit in, they frequently adopt the dominant local language and culture, even if it means denying some of their native culture. Giovanni, a DACA participant, explains, "From the moment I arrived in the United States, I tried my hardest to fit in. I learned English quickly and dropped my Spanish accent. . . . I made friends, consumed popular culture, played video games. . . . I wanted, and often failed, to distance myself from the perception that I did not belong."[21]

"From the moment I arrived in the United States, I tried my hardest to fit in. . . . I wanted, and often failed, to distance myself from the perception that I did not belong."[21]

—Giovanni, DACA recipient

Keeping Secrets

In families that have come here illegally, parents strongly encourage their children to do whatever it takes to fit in—not because they want Dreamers to lose their native culture, but because they believe that blending in will help keep the family's immigration status secret. Indeed, in an effort to keep their undocumented status from being discovered by neighbors, workmates, local law enforcement, or anyone else who might tip off immigration agents, most undocumented immigrants try hard not to draw attention to themselves. And they urge their children to do the same.

Indeed, although many young Dreamers are unaware of or do not understand the meaning of their undocumented status, their parents understand it all too well. They live with the ongoing fear that they will be reported to immigration agents. To protect the family, they instruct young Dreamers not to talk about where they came from and to keep information about the family secret. Some parents even refuse to sign school forms out of fear of being discovered. As a Dreamer named Aylin explains, "I remember occasionally saying I was born here because my parents had always told me to never say I was born in Mexico in fear that someone would get me deported."[22]

Even if young Dreamers do not understand why their parents are afraid, living in an atmosphere filled with anxiety can negatively impact a person's emotional well-being. And as Dreamers mature and come to understand the significance of being undocumented, they deal with the fear of being discovered and deported themselves, as well as the dread of being separated from their families in the process.

A teacher works with a second grade student to help him learn English. Dreamers who live in ethnically diverse communities are often taught by bilingual teachers, and this helps them in school.

Economic Challenges

Many, but not all, young Dreamers also face economic challenges growing up. Unable to work legally, their parents are often forced to work for less pay or in poorer conditions than other workers. In general, employers who hire undocumented workers do not ask for their identity or documentation, do not report their earnings to the government, and might not abide by labor laws. It is not unusual for such employers to take advantage of undocumented workers, demanding that employees work for less than minimum wage under poor working conditions. To make ends meet, the parents of many Dreamers work at multiple jobs. As a result, some young Dreamers do not get to spend much time with their parents. For example, Aylin recalls that when she was growing up, her parents left for work as early as 4:00 a.m. and did not return home until 8:00 p.m. Children in these families often have to take on more household tasks than other young people. They may be responsible for caring for younger siblings, preparing meals, and doing laundry, among other chores.

Plus, many studies indicate that children who are raised in poverty have a heightened risk of developing physical and mental health problems. Lingering infections and dental health issues, for example, can be problems for Dreamers whose families lack health insurance and cannot afford the cost of health care. Under federal law, undocumented immigrants are ineligible for public assistance programs such as food stamps and Medicaid. These programs help low-income Americans support their families and access proper health care. Aylin explains:

> We don't qualify for any services. Growing up, we didn't have any insurance, if we got sick, we'd only go to the doctor if we were dying. We don't go for check-ups or dentist appointments since these services would have to come out of pocket, and there's no money for that. As a child, I would have really bad ear infections where I have to stay home and go through the pain without any medications. My

parents would just have to watch me cry, they didn't have the money to take me to the doctor. The same thing with toothaches. I would have to go through them and so did my parents. Home remedies helped, but it was still painful. Currently, I have a bad TMJ condition where my jaw pops really bad and gets stuck every now and then. I can't do anything. I don't have the money to get the procedure.[23]

Adding to the problem, even when the families of Dreamers can afford medical care, some avoid getting help out of worry that the personal information health care facilities require may get into the hands of immigration agents. For the same reason, they often refrain from reporting crimes. Gladys Klamka, a DACA recipient who was brought to the United States when she was two years old, explains, "At the age of 4 my innocence was stolen from me, I was sexually molested by a 16 year old boy but my parents didn't report it, they didn't understand the law for fear of deportation."[24]

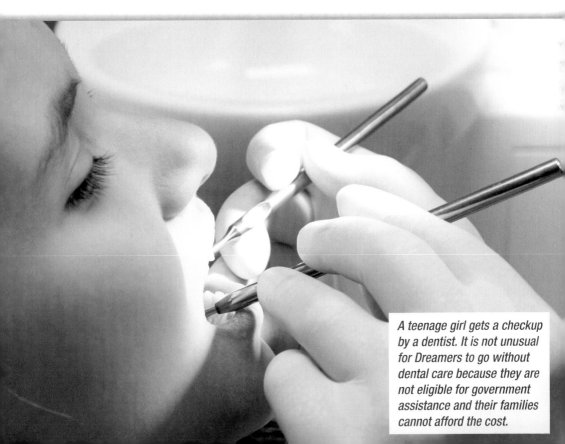

A teenage girl gets a checkup by a dentist. It is not unusual for Dreamers to go without dental care because they are not eligible for government assistance and their families cannot afford the cost.

Becoming Aware

Life becomes more trying for Dreamers once they fully understand the implications of their immigration status. This usually occurs when they are teenagers and discover that many of the privileges and rites of passage that other teens take for granted are prohibited to them. These include getting a driver's license in some states, working legally, or traveling freely (because they may be asked for identification that they do not possess). A Dreamer named Yareli recalls, "I felt like I was trying to grow, but someone was pulling me back simultaneously. Many of the classmates that I knew had legal status, but simply did not want to get a job. This would frustrate me because I would see people around me taking this opportunity for granted while I could not pursue it."[25]

Like their parents, when it comes to work, many Dreamers are forced to work illegally. For instance, in order to finance his post-secondary education, a Dreamer named Carlos took a job cleaning floors and bathrooms in a warehouse and also working as the night watchman. Because of his immigration status, he was paid much less than other workers with similar jobs. And although he knew how to drive, he had to depend on other people to drive him to and from work. When no one was available to do this, like many other Dreamers, he drove illegally, knowing that if he got pulled over for even a tiny infraction, he ran the risk of being detained and deported.

Applying for college is another challenge. In many states, Dreamers do not qualify for in-state tuition and cannot get financial aid or scholarships. Most financial aid and scholarship applications require the applicant to provide a Social Security number, which is not something that undocumented immigrants would normally have. "I remember seeing the list of scholarships to which students could apply and, out of

> "I remember seeing the list of scholarships to which students could apply and, out of the hundreds that were listed, there was only a handful to which I could apply. It was just frustrating."[26]
>
> —Yareli, DACA recipient

Facing Deportation

Without the temporary protections DACA provides, Dreamers face the threat of deportation on a daily basis. Under the Trump administration's immigration policies, ICE agents have been instructed to arrest any undocumented immigrants they encounter, without exception. This includes individuals who have no criminal violations. Therefore, even law-abiding Dreamers who are caught up in immigrant sweeps or raids of workplaces, stores, or neighborhoods by ICE are at risk. Plus, in some cities and states, local police are empowered to enforce immigration laws. Therefore, in these places even a chance encounter with local police can have devastating consequences.

When undocumented individuals are arrested by ICE, they are usually imprisoned and face a court hearing. If the judge approves their deportation, they are transported under armed guards to an exit site, along with other individuals facing deportation. Like hardened criminals, their hands and ankles are cuffed, and their cuffed hands are chained to their waists. They are transported to their country of origin at the US government's expense. They are allowed to take only one small, clear plastic bag holding their belongings with them.

the hundreds that were listed, there was only a handful to which I could apply. It was just frustrating,"[26] Yareli says.

Many Dreamers pin their hopes for a better future on earning a college degree. However, when they learn that their immigration status creates barriers that make paying for college out of reach, their dreams are shattered. A Dreamer named Miriam Ochoa-Garibay recalls, "My parents were very persistent on me getting good grades because that meant a better future. . . . It wasn't until I got to high school where I realized that maybe it was going to take more than just good grades to go to college. I became really aware that I was undocumented, I became fearful that I wasn't going to have a 'better future' because I was undocumented."[27]

Not surprisingly, such experiences cause many Dreamers to sink into depression, which is what happened to a Dreamer named Flor Reyes. She reports, "My high school years were the toughest years of my education. My senior year was my worst year. Depression started to hit me. Everyone was excited to start college. College was something impossible for me."[28]

When faced with these obstacles, some Dreamers become angry with their parents for putting them in this situation in the first place. They may take their anger and frustration out on their parents, only to feel guilty afterward. Barbara Sostaita, a Dreamer, writes, "I recall the times I made my mother cry, blaming her for bringing me to a country that didn't want me and refused

College students attend a lecture. Research has shown that DACA has improved life for many recipients, with about 40 percent of Dreamers earning a bachelor's degree or higher.

to make room for my dreams. I condemned her for bringing me here in the first place. Instead of being angry with a government determined to keep me from thriving, I took it out on her and my dad. I regret those moments wholeheartedly."[29]

DACA Changes Everything

The implementation of DACA changed the lives of many Dreamers. Under DACA, eligible Dreamers no longer had to hide their status or maintain secrets that kept them apart from everyone else. Instead, they could fully integrate into society without fear. They could live like native-born Americans: working and driving legally, traveling, being eligible for in-state tuition and financial aid, and qualifying for bank loans that allowed them to buy homes and cars and start businesses. "With the help of DACA, I have been able to do things and contribute to society in a way I could never have imagined,"[30] explains Hiram, an architect, mentor to young immigrants, and DACA recipient.

Recent surveys show that DACA has improved life for many of the recipients. A 2018 national survey of 1,050 DACA recipients conducted by Tom Wong of the University of California, San Diego, found that 89 percent of respondents were currently employed. Moreover, as a result of their DACA status, 54 percent reported moving to a better-paying job, 46 percent reported moving to a job with better working conditions, and 47 percent reported moving to a job with health insurance. About 40 percent reported pursuing a bachelor's degree or higher.

In other surveys, Dreamers reported that becoming a DACA recipient improved their emotional well-being. Without the threat of deportation hanging over their heads, DACA recipients are less likely to worry about the future. Consequently, they are less likely to suffer from anxiety and depression. For instance, when a Dreamer named Jesus Limón received DACA status, the first

> "I recall the times I made my mother cry, blaming her for bringing me to a country that didn't want me and refused to make room for my dreams. I condemned her for bringing me here in the first place."[29]
>
> —Barbara Sostaita, DACA recipient

thing he did was get his driver's license. He recalls thinking as he drove home from the department of motor vehicles, "This drive home is the first time I don't have to fear being deported."[31]

Lost Dreams

Dreamers' lives were turned upside down again when DACA was rescinded. Even though federal district courts have halted the elimination of the program, uncertainty surrounding the program's future has left DACA recipients in limbo. And it left those who were too young to apply for DACA protection before new applications were halted with little hope for the future. Current DACA recipients worry that if the Supreme Court halts the program entirely and Congress fails to pass another way to protect them, they will lose their legal status and their jobs, in-state tuition, homes, and businesses and will once again face the threat of deportation. They fear it will be easy for immigration agents to identify and locate them based on the information they submitted in order to apply for DACA. In fact, even though DACA applicants were promised that the information they provided would not be shared with ICE, Wong's survey found that only 6.6 percent of respondents reported trusting that the government would keep its promise. "The government knows where we work and where we live. There is no place to hide. There is no living in the shadows anymore. We are living totally exposed and the emotional toll is crushing,"[32] Juan Mendez, a successful business owner and DACA recipient, laments.

Moreover, the loss of DACA would also impact recipients' families. An estimated 25 percent of DACA recipients have young children who were born in the United States. DACA recipients who are parents worry about what will happen to their children if they are deported. Children who are old

> "The government knows where we work and where we live. There is no place to hide. There is no living in the shadows anymore. We are living totally exposed and the emotional toll is crushing."[32]
>
> —Juan Mendez, DACA recipient

Getting a Driver's License

Getting a driver's license is a major milestone for most teens. The rules related to undocumented immigrants obtaining a driver's license differ from state to state. Currently, all fifty states allow DACA participants to get a driver's license. Non-DACA recipients and other undocumented immigrants are prohibited from obtaining a driver's license in thirty-eight states. In these states, if a Dreamer's deferred action protection expires, so does his or her driver's license.

Twelve states—California, Colorado, Connecticut, Delaware, Hawaii, Illinois, Maryland, Nevada, New Mexico, Utah, Vermont, and Washington, plus the District of Columbia and Puerto Rico—allow all eligible residents to obtain a driver's license, no matter their immigration status. In these states undocumented individuals are issued a non–Real ID compliant driver's license, while US citizens qualify for a Real ID compliant license. A Real ID compliant license is accepted for official federal identification purposes, while a non–Real ID compliant license is not.

Under the Real ID Act, which is a federal law aimed at improving national security, starting in October 2020, a Real ID compliant license or another acceptable form of identification such as a valid passport, US military ID, or federal government personal identification verification card, will be required to enter most federal facilities and to board an airplane. Therefore, all states, including those that do not issue driver's licenses to undocumented people, must change their licensing process and issue Real ID compliant licenses. DACA recipients can get a temporary Real ID compliant driver's license.

enough to understand this situation worry about being separated from their parents as well.

Dreamers' worries do not end there. Even if the Supreme Court rules that DACA is legal, many Dreamers fear that the administration will find another way to dismantle it, and whatever rights they are given will be taken away again. Plus, DACA was always meant as a temporary fix. It does not provide Dreamers a path to citizenship as a Dream Act would. And that is what Dreamers want most of all.

Chapter Four

Differing Views

Americans have differing views about the Dreamers, their plight, and their impact on society. Multiple polls indicate that the majority of Americans favor protecting the Dreamers. For instance, a 2018 National Public Radio poll of 1,004 randomly selected Americans found that 65 percent of the respondents support giving Dreamers legal status. But there are many individuals who feel otherwise. Both sides offer a variety of reasons to defend their point of view. Some of these reasons are rooted in facts, while others are based on misinformation. No matter the basis of these views, such views impact Dreamers' lives.

Viewing Dreamers as Lawbreakers

According to federal laws, foreigners who enter the United States outside of a legal port of entry or elude examination by an immigration agent can be charged with a criminal misdemeanor, which is punishable by a fine, detention, and deportation. Similarly, undocumented immigrants who are unlawfully present in the United States, even if they initially entered the country legally, are deemed lawbreakers who committed a civil violation that is punishable by deportation. Current laws do not distinguish between adults who knowingly violated immigration laws and children who had no control over such decisions. Based on these laws, many Americans view and treat all unauthorized immigrants, even those who were brought here as children, as wrongdoers. Being viewed and treated disapprovingly is frustrating and upsetting to many law-abiding Dreamers. It makes them feel ashamed, as if they are inferior to American citizens and individuals with legal resident status. Astrid, a Dreamer who came to the United States from Mexico when she was four years old, explains, "I have never, ever as much as stolen even a piece of gum, but I feel like a criminal."[33]

Most of those who view the Dreamers as lawbreakers take an absolutist view on illegal immigration. They contend that all immigration laws should be enforced without exception. In their judgment the fact that Dreamers broke the law through no fault of their own does not excuse the end result. In their view all unauthorized immigrants are lawbreakers, no matter their backstory. Jennifer Sullivan, a member of the Florida House of Representatives, explains, "I feel like . . . something has gotten lost that is a crucial, main point. And that is the fact that we're talking about people who are here illegally. That means that, legally, they are breaking the law."[34]

Consequently, some Americans oppose the passage of a Dream Act and the continuation of DACA. They believe that giving Dreamers the opportunity to work, the chance to attend college while paying in-state tuition, and a path to citizenship rewards misconduct and undermines the rule of law.

Children Had No Choice

In contrast, other Americans make a distinction between the Dreamers and other unauthorized immigrants. They maintain that the Dreamers are a special group who are innocent of any wrongdoing since, as minors, they had no control over their

"I feel like . . . something has gotten lost that is a crucial, main point. And that is the fact that we're talking about people who are here illegally. That means that, legally, they are breaking the law."[34]

—Jennifer Sullivan, member of the Florida House of Representatives

Americans Support Legal Status for Dreamers

Despite having mixed views on illegal immigration, Americans over-whelmingly support permanent legal status for undocumented immigrants who were brought to the United States as children. Even when responses are broken down by political party, support for this action is high—especially among Democrats and Democratic-leaning independents but also among Republicans and Republican-leaning independents.

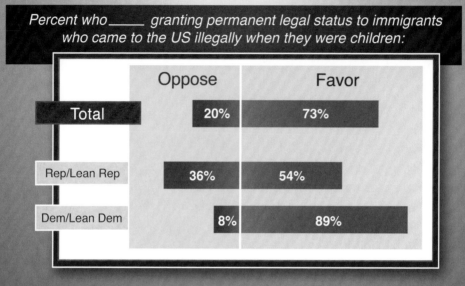

Percent who_____ granting permanent legal status to immigrants who came to the US illegally when they were children:

	Oppose	Favor
Total	20%	73%
Rep/Lean Rep	36%	54%
Dem/Lean Dem	8%	89%

Note: Do Not Know responses are not shown

Source: Carroll Doherty, "Americans Broadly Support Legal Status for Immigrants Brought to the U.S. Illegally as Children," Pew Research Center, June 18, 2018. www.pewresearch.org.

parents' choices. Writer and college student Sasha Vassilyeva explains:

> As a child, your life is controlled by the adults that are in it. Everything you do, everything you wear, everywhere you go is decided by your caretakers. . . . Immigrant children seldom have a choice when it comes to leaving one country to go to another, let alone whether or not it will be done legally. As a minor, you rely on your parents to get you the legal status that you need to thrive in this country. But when parents don't take action, what can children do? The answer is simple: nothing. . . . It's the parents who chose

to come here and to do so illegally. . . . The Dreamers had no say in the decision to come to the United States, so why should they be punished?[35]

Most of these individuals want to protect the Dreamers from the threat of deportation by offering them a path to citizenship. Many also believe that it is cruel and immoral to do otherwise. Thiru Vignarajah, a lawyer, politician, and former deputy attorney general of Maryland, writes:

> To deport immigrants raised in America since they were children for the supposed sins of their parents is the definition of cruel and unusual punishment—expelling a person to a country they do not know because of a decision they did not make is as spiteful as it is bizarre. . . . To separate someone from friends and family and to end the life they have built in America—unthinkable consequences for the actions of another—are as cruel and unusual a punishment as one can conceive.[36]

Does DACA Encourage Illegal Immigration?

The Dreamers and the laws intended to help them are not always viewed in such stark terms. Some Americans express sympathy for the plight of the Dreamers while also worrying that laws intended to help them will encourage more illegal immigration. Word of deferred deportations or offers of a path to citizenship could be a strong lure for others who are contemplating illegal entry. Such policies could lead to a surge of unauthorized immigrant parents bringing their children across the border in

"To deport immigrants raised in America since they were children for the supposed sins of their parents is the definition of cruel and unusual punishment—expelling a person to a country they do not know because of a decision they did not make is as spiteful as it is bizarre."[36]

—Thiru Vignarajah, a lawyer, politician, and former deputy attorney general of Maryland hopes of gaining similar benefits for them. Conservative speech-writer Robert Heiler understands these concerns because he shares them. He explains, "The truth is that most people's view of DACA is conflicted. They understand and sympathize with the plight of the Dreamers; but they also know that the biggest problem in U.S. immigration policy is the existence of a perverse regime of incentives, which actually encourages what it claims to criminalize."[37]

Some take this argument even further. Ira Mehlman is media director for the Federation for American Immigration Reform, a group that favors more stringent immigration laws. Mehlman believes that, over time, the plight of new arrivals will mirror that of the original Dreamers, which will arouse the sympathy of many Americans. As a result, these policies will be amended, new entrants will be grandfathered in, and more people will come

A group of Central American refugees turn themselves in to the Texas Border Patrol. When DACA was first established, a surge of immigrants from Central America tried to cross the Mexico-US border.

in hopes of attaining the same outcomes for their children. He contends:

> If we have a moral imperative to provide amnesty to the current population of people who were brought here as kids, won't we have the same moral imperative for the next generation of people who arrive under similar circumstances? The unmistakable message to people all around the world is: Get over here and bring your kids. America will feel morally obligated to give them green cards too.[38]

Doing the Right Thing

Others argue that DACA and the various proposed versions of the Dream Act all clearly set limits on eligibility. They contend that because these bills only apply to unauthorized individuals who are already in the country, the magnet effect will be minimal. Data compiled by the border patrol suggests they may be correct. In 2012, the year DACA was established, there was a surge of unaccompanied minors and immigrant families from Central America crossing the southern border without authorization. However, the surge occurred entirely in the months before the policy was announced. Another surge occurred in 2014. Most immigration analysts maintain that both these surges occurred in reaction to increased violence and worsening economic conditions in Central America at the time. DACA, they said, was not a contributing factor in either surge.

But even if potential migrants misunderstand these policies and attempt to take advantage of them, many Americans

"If we have a moral imperative to provide amnesty to the current population of people who were brought here as kids, won't we have the same moral imperative for the next generation of people who arrive under similar circumstances?"[38]

—Ira Mehlman, media director for the Federation for American Immigration Reform say that concerns about future unauthorized immigration should not prevent the United States from doing the right thing by those who are here now. A DACA recipient currently employed by IBM writes:

> I hope Members of Congress can pass legislation to give Dreamers like me certainty that our entire lives won't be taken away from us in the blink of an eye. We've worked hard. We've overcome adversity, and we've found a way to give back to our communities, to the economy and to the country that has been our home for as long as we can remember. This country hasn't let me down yet, and I am hopeful that leaders in Washington won't let us down either.[39]

Impact on Jobs and Workers

The impact of granting legal status and eventual citizenship to Dreamers also inspires a mix of views on the topic of jobs and American workers. It seems logical to assume that more immigrant workers will mean fewer jobs for Americans. This fear is not new. It is a constant topic in debates over US immigration policies going back decades. The specter of lost jobs was again raised in 2017 when attorney general Jeff Sessions announced Trump's decision to end DACA. Sessions stated that DACA beneficiaries have taken jobs away from hundreds of thousands of Americans.

Some top economists say that this claim has no basis in fact and that fears of DACA recipients replacing American workers are unfounded. In fact, many DACA recipients are well educated and help fill needs in high-demand areas such as health care, education, and social services. According to the National Education Association, close to nine thousand Dreamers are educators, many in the field of bilingual education, an area of significant shortages. Plus, many Dreamers speak more than one language and are familiar with diverse cultures. These are skills that are in high demand in the global economy.

Crime and Dreamers

In speeches and articles, Trump, members of his administration, various conservative politicians, and members of anti-immigration groups have alleged that undocumented immigrants, including Dreamers, bring crime and violence to the United States. A 2017 report by the nonpartisan Cato Institute shows that this is not the case. Using statistics gathered by the US Census Bureau's American Community Survey, the Cato Institute concludes that Dreamers are actually less likely to commit crimes than native-born Americans. In comparing the two groups, the researchers found that Dreamers make up about 2.05 percent of the total US population but only 1.94 percent of the total prison population. American citizens in the same age group make up 87.19 percent of the population but are 94.84 percent of all prisoners.

In total, the report goes on to explain, the incarceration rate for native-born Americans is 14 percent higher than that of Dreamers. Therefore, the report concludes, "Despite individual news stories and anecdotes to the contrary, DREAMers are less crime prone than native-born Americans."

Michelangelo Landgrave and Alex Nowrasteh, "The DREAMer Incarceration Rate," Cato Institute, August 30, 2017. www.cato.org.

Moreover, as of May 2019 the US unemployment rate was 3.6 percent, the lowest in fifty years. This translates to over 6 million job openings across all career fields. In this type of job market, it is unlikely that Dreamers are crowding out American workers. Ray Perryman, president and chief executive officer of Texas economic research firm the Perryman Group, says, "I think the primary thing that would argue against [Sessions's claim] at this point is, we are at full employment with more job openings than at any point in history. We desperately need workers in this country."[40]

In addition, as a country's population grows, so does the demand for housing, food, and other goods and services, as well as for workers to build the houses, grow and sell the food, and so forth. Consequently, in a sense, by their very presence Dreamers create jobs for Americans. Dreamers also help create jobs by starting their own businesses and hiring people to work in those businesses. A 2017 survey of DACA recipients indicates that 5.6 percent have started their own businesses. Dreamers have started real estate agencies, artificial intelligence companies, construction businesses, photography studios, stores, and restaurants, among other businesses. A Dreamer named Mostafa, for example, is part of this group. He started a New York City event-staffing business that has grown from a small operation to a business that employs about thirty people.

Taking or Contributing?

How Dreamers impact other aspects of the economy is also controversial. Some Americans maintain that the Dreamers take more from the economy than they contribute. They argue that Dreamers strain local, state, and federal coffers by using public utilities and transportation, attending public schools, and receiving costly social services such as Medicaid, food stamps, and Social Security without paying taxes that fund these types of programs.

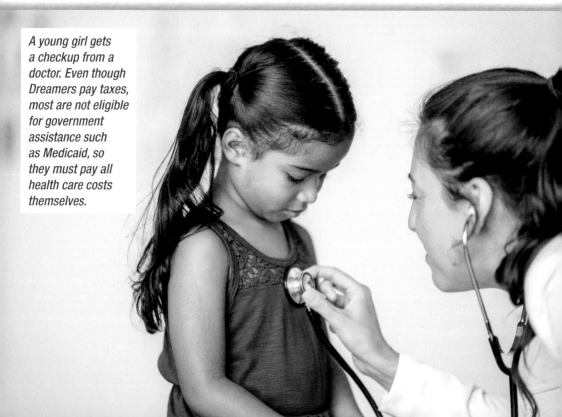

A young girl gets a checkup from a doctor. Even though Dreamers pay taxes, most are not eligible for government assistance such as Medicaid, so they must pay all health care costs themselves.

The Financial Impact of DACA

Although some Americans contend that DACA puts a strain on the economy, a 2017 survey conducted by Tom Wong of the University of California, San Diego, of DACA recipients suggests otherwise. DACA has enabled recipients to find jobs, earn higher wages, buy cars, and in some cases, even buy homes. All of this activity contributes to the economy. According to the survey, only 44 percent of the respondents were employed before becoming DACA recipients. After implementation of DACA, 91 percent of recipients under age twenty-five and 93 percent of recipients over age twenty-five had jobs. Moreover, after receiving DACA, respondents' average hourly wage increased by nearly 70 percent.

Their improved financial well-being has allowed DACA participants to contribute more to the economy. According to the survey, 60 percent of respondents reported opening their first bank account and getting their first credit card after becoming a DACA recipient. Sixty-six percent of respondents purchased their first car, and 16 percent bought their first home.

The idea that Dreamers take unfair advantage of governmental services is, according to experts, a misconception. Most Dreamers are not eligible for social assistance programs even though they pay income, sales, and other taxes that help fund these programs. Under federal law anyone who earns an income in the United States—including unauthorized immigrants—is required to file a tax return and pay income taxes. Those without a Social Security number are assigned a tax processing number to identify themselves. Although some individuals working in the informal cash economy do not report their earnings to the government, most Dreamers who work in the informal economy comply with the law. Doing so helps verify their good moral character and documents their employment history and continuous residency in the United States. These factors can help them gain DACA status or legal permanent resident status in the future.

In addition, payroll taxes and deductions for Social Security and Medicare are automatically taken out of the paychecks of

Dreamers working in the formal labor market. According to the National Immigration Forum, an immigrant advocacy organization, in the period from 2017 to 2027, DACA recipients are projected to contribute an estimated $12.3 billion in taxes to Social Security and Medicare for services they are prohibited from receiving. Javi, a DACA recipient and blogger, explains, "For the past two years I paid more than $1,400 in taxes and have never used unemployment services, welfare, food stamps, or any other type of government assistance."[41]

Dreamers also contribute to the economy by paying state and local income and sales taxes. The Economic Policy Institute, a nonpartisan tax policy organization, reports that as a group, Dreamers and other unauthorized immigrants pay more than $7 billion in sales taxes annually. This money helps fund public utilities, transportation, roads, and local school districts, which Dreamers also use.

Facts Matter

Clearly, Americans have differing views about the Dreamers and their impact on society. Some of these views are based on facts and some falsehoods or fears. Briyit, a DACA recipient and nursing student, tries to add an air of reality to a conversation that at times seems to spin out of control:

> We are not criminals, as many quote us to be, we are not parasites. With DACA, yes, we are given a work permit, and technically, the same advantages as any other citizen has. The only difference is we do not get handpicks [government assistant services]. So for instance, because we are working, they take the taxes away, but we are not able to get FAFSA [Free Application for Federal Student Aid] or health insurance. So I want to encourage people to educate themselves before they take a stand.[42]

Chapter Five

What the Future Holds

Democratic and Repub-
lican lawmakers agree that
immigration laws need to be
reformed and that issues concern-
ing the Dreamers and DACA should
be addressed. But there has been little
agreement on what changes to make. In this
environment of uncertainty, Dreamers have decided to speak out and to stand up for themselves.
They have tried to increase public awareness of their
plight and to urge enactment of laws that will allow them to
plan for their futures. Juan, a Dreamer activist, avows, "We will
fight back. We will organize and create our own narrative and
not allow them [conservative politicians] to create one for us.
. . . We can't stay quiet."[43]

More Dream Acts Proposed

One of the things Dreamer activists are fighting for is passage
of a Dream Act. During 2019 two versions of the Dream Act
were introduced in Congress. On June 4, 2019, the House
passed the American Dream and Promise Act by a vote of
237 to 187. The vote was along political party lines, with
Democrats supporting the measure and most Republicans
opposing it. The bill gives eligible Dreamers access to in-state
college tuition and federal student financial aid and provides
them with a path to citizenship. To be covered under the bill,
Dreamer applicants must meet similar requirements to those
proposed in earlier versions of the Dream Act.

In addition to protecting Dreamers, the American Dream
and Promise Act gives legal permanent residency status to

eligible immigrants covered under two other programs: Temporary Protective Status (TPS) and the Deferred Enforcement Departure (DED). These programs allow eligible immigrants who are already in the United States and who come from certain designated countries interim legal status. This status can be granted based on dangerous temporary conditions in their native country that prevent them from safely returning. When the status expires, it may be extended if conditions in the native country remain unsafe. Qualifying conditions include natural disasters, armed conflict, and epidemics. Because of ongoing problems in some of the designated countries, many of these individuals have lived in the United States for more than a decade. As with DACA, the Trump administration is phasing out TPS and DED. It will stop granting TPS and DED status to immigrants from seven countries by January 2020, putting approximately four hundred thousand individuals at risk of deportation.

House approval of the American Dream and Promise Act did not make it law. For any bill to become law, it must also be approved by the Senate and signed by the president. As of the fall of 2019, this outcome seemed unlikely. On June 5, 2019, one day after the House passed the American Dream and Promise Act, Republican Senate majority leader Mitch McConnell said that the bill would probably never be brought up for a vote in the Senate. What is more, Trump threatened to veto it if it passed. McConnell seemed to be holding out for reforms that went beyond the needs of the Dreamers. "The Dreamers have a sympathetic case. There are circumstances under which I and others would be happy to support that," McConnell said. "But we need to do more than that. You know there's some genuine fixes on the legal

"The Dreamers have a sympathetic case. There are circumstances under which I and others would be happy to support that. But we need to do more than that. You know there's some genuine fixes on the legal immigration side and on the illegal immigration side that need to be addressed."[44]

—Mitch McConnell, Senate majority leader

House speaker Nancy Pelosi (pictured) talks during an event in support of the American Dream and Promise Act. In June 2019, the House passed the act with Democrats supporting it and most Republicans opposed.

DREAM & PROMISE ACT OF 2019
#ProtectTheDream

immigration side and on the illegal immigration side that need to be addressed."[44]

A separate bill, the Dream Act of 2019, was introduced in the Senate on March 26, 2019. It is similar to the House bill. According to political experts, the Senate bill had about as much chance of becoming law as the House one did.

The States Take Action

In the absence of action by Congress and the president, states are taking their own steps to protect Dreamers. As of 2019 twenty-one states had passed state Dream Acts, and other states were considering adoption of similar laws. The specific provisions of these acts vary from state to state. However, the primary focus is education. In general, state Dream Acts allow eligible Dreamers to pay in-state tuition at public colleges in the

United We Dream

Organizations like United We Dream, which was established by Dreamers, help train and inspire other Dreamers to advocate for themselves. An article on the organization's website describes its purpose in this way:

> When you're undocumented, you face a lot of discrimination, and that creates a lot of fear. At United We Dream, we transform that fear into finding your voice. We empower people to develop their leadership, their organizing skills, and to develop our own campaigns to fight for justice and dignity for immigrants and all people. This is achieved through immigrant youth-led campaigns at the local, state, and federal level. . . . We create welcoming spaces for young people—regardless of immigration status—to support, engage, and empower them to make their voice heard and win! . . . We are made up of fearless youth fighting to improve the lives of ourselves, our families and our communities. Our vision is a society which celebrates our diversity. . . . Whether we're organizing in the streets, building cutting edge technology systems, opening doors for LGBTQ immigrant youth, clearing pathways to education, stopping deportations or creating alliances across social movements, United We Dream puts undocumented immigrant youth in the driver's seat to strategize, innovate and win.

United We Dream, "About UWD," 2018. https://unitedwedream.org.

state in which they reside. In addition, as of 2019 seven states (California, Minnesota, New Mexico, New York, Oregon, Texas, and Washington) also allow eligible Dreamers to qualify for state-funded student financial aid.

By allowing Dreamers to pay in-state tuition rates and obtain financial assistance that they would otherwise be ineligible for, state Dream Acts make it possible for more Dreamers to further their education. State Dream Acts, however, do not override federal immigration laws. Therefore, they do not address or impact Dreamers' immigration status, provide them with work permits, or shield them from deportation.

While some states are trying to support the Dreamers, other states have passed or are proposing laws that do just the opposite. For example, Georgia prohibits undocumented immigrants, including DACA recipients, from attending its top five public universities. Alabama and South Carolina ban Dreamers who do not have DACA status from applying to any public postsecondary institution. Georgia, Arizona, and Indiana also prohibit DACA recipients from receiving in-state tuition rates. Instead, they must pay out-of-state tuition rates that are about three times higher than in-state tuition.

Dreamers in Arizona have experienced yet another change. Until recently, eligible DACA recipients residing in Arizona qualified for in-state tuition at public colleges. But in April 2018 the Arizona Supreme Court ruled that this violates a state law that requires foreign-born students to have lawful immigration status to qualify for in-state tuition. According to the US Citizenship and Immigration Services, DACA recipients are classified as "lawfully present," which, the court ruled, does not match state law. As a result, tuition for DACA students was set to increase by at least 150 percent. The ruling, which was enacted in 2018, affects an estimated two thousand DACA students enrolled in Arizona public colleges, as well as those hoping to enroll in the future. For example, Pablo, a DACA recipient, was in his final semester at Phoenix Community College when the new law was enacted. He had planned to continue his education at Arizona State University (ASU) but now doubts he will be able to do so. "My goals of attending Arizona State University are now falling apart," he says. "It's not affordable. . . . I don't see a way for me to finish my other two years and obtain my bachelor's from ASU."[45]

Support from Diverse Sources

With so much at stake, a diverse group of individuals representing businesses, labor unions, the arts, government, religious organizations, and education have come out in support of the Dreamers. They, along with many other Americans, join Dreamer activists in peaceful marches, sit-ins, and rallies; express their views on social media and other media outlets; and lobby local, state, and federal lawmakers. According to the Center for Responsive Politics, a nonpartisan think tank, in 2017 and 2018 close to four hundred groups lobbied lawmakers in support of DACA and the Dream Act. Among Dreamer supporters are executives representing tech companies like Facebook, Apple, and Microsoft. In the past two years, an organization that a group of tech leaders founded has spent more than $1.6 million lobbying in support of the Dreamers.

Support comes from other sources, too. In fact, many individuals and groups backing the Dreamers have widely differing views on other political issues but are in agreement when it comes to protecting the Dreamers. Among these are individuals representing Walmart, Koch Industries, Starbucks, the Sierra Club, and the Catholic Church. Other strong support comes from the National Retail Federation, the National Restaurant Association, Hewlett-Packard, IBM, and General Motors, among many others. In fact,

Many Americans have spoken out on behalf of Dreamers and have supported them in numerous ways, such as participating in peaceful marches, sit-ins, and rallies; expressing their views on social media; and lobbying lawmakers.

after the Trump administration announced DACA's rescission, executives from hundreds of companies across all career fields sent a letter to the president asking him to rethink his decision. The letter also urged lawmakers to pass a Dream Act or similar legislation that would protect the Dreamers. In the August 2017 letter, the executives wrote, "Dreamers are vital to the future of our companies and our economy. With them, we grow and create jobs. They are part of why we will continue to have a global competitive advantage."[46]

In addition, more than seventy-five universities, the National Education Association, and educational leaders throughout the country have thrown their support behind the Dreamers. Since 2017 the University of California system alone has spent nearly $2.3 million lobbying for immigration-related issues and defending DACA in court. School district representatives, too, have spoken out. Florida's Miami-Dade school superintendent Alberto Calvalho says, "There is nothing more right than for our community here and beyond to stand up, to show up, to speak up, to close arms around our children who are Americans in every single way but one. They were not born here. . . . It's important that we send a message to the White House. The message is clear. These men and women are our future. Please protect them."[47]

Many celebrities are also trying to help the Dreamers. They have participated in marches and rallies and have posted messages to lawmakers and Trump on social media in support of DACA and the passage of a Dream Act. Notables such as Snoop Dogg, Gigi Hadid, Cher, Mark Ruffalo, and Elizabeth Banks have publicly backed the Dreamers. So have Ellen DeGeneres, Brie Larson, America Ferrera, Bradley Whitford, and Alyssa Milano, just to name a few. In fact, in 2018 Ferrera, Milano, and Whitford organized a protest and press conference at the office of California senator Dianne Feinstein

"There is nothing more right than for our community here and beyond to stand up, to show up, to speak up, to close arms around our children who are Americans in every single way but one. They were not born here."[47]

—Alberto Calvalho, superintendent of Miami-Dade County Public Schools in support of the Dreamers and the passage of a Dream Act. Milano has also tweeted her support for the Dreamers directly to Trump. She explains, "It's not what you look like or where you were born, that makes you American. . . . America is at its best when it embraces the ideal that all people are created equal. How we treat DREAMers reflects our commitment to the values that define us as Americans."[48]

"America is at its best when it embraces the ideal that all people are created equal. How we treat DREAMers reflects our commitment to the values that define us as Americans."[48]

—Alyssa Milano, actress and activist

Dreamer Activists

Most of this support can be attributed to the efforts of Dreamer activists. These young men and women have put themselves and their loved ones at risk of deportation by coming out of the shadows in order to raise the spotlight on their situation and advocate for legislation that changes current immigration policies. Taking a cue from the civil rights and gay rights movements, Dreamers from all over the United States have formed a large and powerful network of national organizations such as United We Dream, National Immigrant Youth Alliance, and DreamACTivist, among other national, state, and local groups.

These groups stage peaceful demonstrations and rallies; hold sit-ins in courthouses, immigrant detention facilities, and ICE and lawmakers' offices; build alliances with powerful supporters; meet with lawmakers; and connect Dreamers via social media. They aim to empower Dreamers by educating them about their rights and training them to be leaders in their communities. They also use art, film, and music to get their message across. It is partially due to pressure from Dreamer activists who met with President Obama that DACA was established in 2012. "It was incredible, almost surreal, to see the power we had to make the president act,"[49] Dreamer activist Julieta Garibay recalls.

What is more, within hours after the rescission of DACA was announced in 2017, Dreamer activists launched a protest in front of the White House, blocking traffic in nearby streets. Others organized a sit-in in front of Trump Tower in New York, where at least thirty-four protesters were arrested. At the same time, high school students in Denver, Phoenix, and Albuquerque, among other cities, walked out of class. The next day, other activists dressed in business suits and marched through the lobby of the Trump International Hotel in Washington, DC, shouting, "Here to stay!"[50]

A few months later, in November 2017 an estimated two thousand Dreamers and their supporters marched to the Capitol building in Washington, DC, demanding that legislators pass a Dream Act. Other Dreamers staged walkouts and rallies all over the United States in support of the marchers.

Dreamer activist Julieta Garibay, director of the United We Dream campaign, is shown in her Washington, DC, office. Garibay and other activists were instrumental in the original creation of DACA in 2012.

These kinds of activities are ongoing. For instance, in 2018 Dream activists once again marched on the Capitol in an attempt to get Congress to pass laws to protect them. Some of the protestors chained themselves to one another, closing off nearby streets to traffic, and eighty-six were arrested. The activists also arranged flowers on the grass around the Capitol, spelling out "unafraid" in big letters that legislators could see from their office windows. Then in 2019 Dreamer activists met with and lobbied legislators, held rallies, and organized a letter-writing campaign urging members of Congress to pass the American Dream and Promise Act.

Dreamer Activists Use the Arts to Raise Public Awareness

While many Dreamer activists and their supporters are lobbying lawmakers and taking part in peaceful demonstrations, others are using the arts to advocate for their cause. For example, in 2019 an album entitled *American Dreamers, Voices of Hope, Music of Freedom* won three Grammy Awards. The album was performed by jazz trumpeter John Daversa and a big band made up of fifty-three Dreamers. The Dreamers, who were born in seventeen different countries and live in seventeen different states, came together to show their love for the United States by playing and singing songs about America and freedom.

Other Dreamers have formed a group known as Dreamers Adrift. They create videos, films, music, art, and poetry in an effort to raise public awareness of what it means to be undocumented and gain support for the passage of a Dream Act. The group has made more than ninety videos, including two original YouTube series, *Undocumented & Awkward* and *Osito, Jesús, and Julio.*

Julio Salgado, a cofounder of Dreamers Adrift, calls himself an "artivist." He has gained renown as a visual artist. As a gay Dreamer, Salgado's posters and other artwork help empower and raise the spotlight on LGBTQ Dreamers. His work also includes messages in support of the enactment of a Dream Act and in opposition to anti-immigration laws. Prints of his work are often carried by Dreamer activists and their supporters in rallies and demonstrations.

Many were present in the Capitol building on the day the bill was passed in the House of Representatives. And although they are not eligible to vote, Dreamers are also busily working on local, state, and national elections. They are speaking to groups, making phone calls, posting on social media, and going door-to-door in an effort to get candidates who support their agenda elected. In fact, Dreamers served as Latino vote coordinators in both Hillary Clinton's and Bernie Sanders's 2016 presidential campaigns.

By coming forward to fight for their rights, Dreamer activists become targets for reprisal by immigration authorities—as do their loved ones. Yet these courageous individuals refuse to be cowed. As Nebraska Dreamer activist Armando Becerril Sierra wrote in an op-ed column in the *Lincoln Journal Star*, "The easy thing to do would be to lay low. . . . Nevertheless, my fellow Dreamers, our allies and I will continue to work for what is right and just, so others can pursue their own American dream."[51]

"The easy thing to do would be to lay low. . . . Nevertheless, my fellow Dreamers, our allies and I will continue to work for what is right and just, so others can pursue their own American dream."[51]

—Armando Becerril Sierra, Dreamer activist

Introduction: American in All Ways but One

1. Quoted in Faces of DACA, "Luis's Journey," September 30, 2017. www.facesofdaca.us.
2. Quoted in Faces of DACA, "Luis's Journey."
3. Quoted in Faces of DACA, "Luis's Journey."
4. Quoted in Kameron Schmid and Joseph Daniels, "Faces of DACA at Sac State," *State Hornet*, October 5, 2017. https://statehornet.com.

Chapter One: Changing Policies

5. William A. Schwab, *Right to Dream*. Fayetteville: University of Arkansas Press, 2013, p. 62.
6. *Addressing the Immigration Status of Illegal Immigrants Brought to the United States as Children, Before the Subcommittee on Immigration and Border Security, Committee on the Judiciary*, US House of Representatives (2013) (statement of Senator Cory Gardner).
7. Quoted in Eileen Truax, *Dreamers: An Immigrant Generation's Fight for Their American Dream*. Boston: Beacon, 2015, p. 55.
8. Laura Wides-Muñoz, *The Making of a Dream*. New York: HarperCollins, 2018, p. 217.
9. Quoted in Ed Escoto, *Dreamers Have a Dream Too*. CreateSpace, 2017, p. 25.
10. Quoted in Kaitlan Collins, "Candidate Trump Promised to Terminate DACA. President Trump Says Dreamers Can 'Rest Easy,'" Daily Caller, April 21, 2017. https://dailycaller.com.
11. Quoted in Mark Joseph Stern, "The 'Judicial Resistance' Didn't Save DACA," Slate, April 27, 2018. https://slate.com.
12. Quoted in Schmid and Daniels, "Faces of DACA at Sac State."
13. Quoted in Annie Karni and Sheryl Gay Stolberg, "Trump Offers Temporary Protection for 'Dreamers' in Exchange for Wall Funding," *New York Times*, January 19, 2019. www.nytimes.com.

14. Quoted in Max Bryan, "Fort Smith DACA Recipient Feels like 'Political Football,'" *Fort Smith (AR) Times Record*, January 24, 2018. www.swtimes.com.

Chapter Two: Who Are the Dreamers?

15. Alma Aparicio, "Alma Aparicio," Define American, 2019. https://defineamerican.com.
16. Quoted in Michelle Kanaar, "Who Are Chicago's Dreamers? Here Are the Faces of DACA," *Chicago Reader*, March 1, 2018. www.chicagoreader.com.
17. Quoted in Faces of DACA, "Rosie's Journey," October 31, 2017. www.facesofdaca.us.
18. Kirk W. Johnson, "A DACA Recipient with an American Life Considers the Future," *New Yorker*, September 13, 2017. www.newyorker.com.
19. Quoted in Bryan, "Fort Smith DACA Recipient Feels like 'Political Football.'"
20. Leezia Dhalla, "DACA Is Not a Free Pass for Dreamers Like Me," *Self*, September 6, 2017. www.self.com.

Chapter Three: Many Challenges

21. Giovanni, "Giovanni," *New York Times*. www.nytimes.com.
22. Quoted in Faces of DACA, "Aylin's Journey," October 7, 2017. www.facesofdaca.us.
23. Quoted in Faces of DACA, "Aylin's Journey."
24. Gladys Klamka, "Gladys Klamka," *New York Times*. www.nytimes.com.
25. Quoted in Faces of DACA, "Yareli's Journey," September 16, 2017. www.facesofdaca.us.
26. Quoted in Faces of DACA, "Yareli's Journey."
27. Miriam Ochoa-Garibay, "Miriam Ochoa-Garibay," *New York Times*. www.nytimes.com.
28. Flor Reyes, "Flor Reyes," *New York Times*. www.nytimes.com.
29. Quoted in Jasmine Garsd, "Coming to America: A Mistake? Many Parents of DACA Recipients Are Wondering," PRI, September 8, 2017. www.pri.org.
30. Quoted in Escoto, *Dreamers Have a Dream Too*, p. 26.

31. Quoted in Schmid and Daniels, "Faces of DACA at Sac State."
32. Quoted in William A. Schwab, *Dreams Derailed*. Fayetteville: University of Arkansas Press, 2019, p. 104.

Chapter Four: Differing Views

33. Quoted in Wides-Muñoz, *The Making of a Dream*, p. 144.
34. Quoted in Louis Jacobson, "Is Being in the United States Unlawfully a 'Crime'?," PolitiFact, March 15, 2017. www.politi fact.com.
35. Sasha Vassilyeva, "Dreamers Shouldn't Be Punished for Their Parents' Choices," *Loyola Phoenix*, September 12, 2017. http://loyolaphoenix.com.
36. Thiru Vignarajah, "Deporting Dreamers Is as Cruel and Unusual as It Gets," *Seattle Times*, November 12, 2017. www .seattletimes.com.
37. Robert Heiler, "Deconstructing the DACA Debate," Real Clear Politics, September 8, 2017. www.realclearpolitics.com.
38. Ira Mehlman, "Five Moral Arguments Against the Dream Act," Townhall, July 1, 2011. https://townhall.com.
39. Quoted in IBM, "Dreamers: The Only Life I've Ever Known," October 24, 2017. www.ibm.com.
40. Quoted in Danielle Kurtzleben, "Fact Check: Are DACA Recipients Stealing Jobs Away from Other Americans?," NPR, September 6, 2017. https://npr.org.
41. Javi, "Here's How Much DACA Recipients Pay into the Economy," Dreamer Money, August 10, 2018. https://dreamer money.com.
42. Quoted in Kanaar, "Who Are Chicago's Dreamers?"

Chapter Five: What the Future Holds

43. Quoted in Schwab, *Dreams Derailed*, p. 104.
44. Quoted in Burgess Everett, "McConnell: Senate Will 'Probably Not' Vote on Dreamers Bill," Politico, June 5, 2019. www .politico.com.
45. Quoted in Chris McCrory, "DACA Advocates Frustrated at Ruling Against In-State Tuition for 'Dreamers,'" AZ Central, April 9, 2018. www.azcentral.com.

46. Quoted in Tracy Jan, "Hundreds of Business Leaders Call on Trump to Protect 'Dreamers,'" *Washington Post*, September 1, 2017. www.washingtonpost.com.

47. Quoted in Alex Harris and Kyra Gurney, "Miami Leaders Line Up to Support Dreamers and Ask Trump to Do the Right Thing," *Miami Herald*, August 31, 2017. www.miamiherald.com.

48. Quoted in Now This, "Alyssa Milano, Piper Perabo, Activists Team Up to Pass DREAM Act Now," January 11, 2018. https://nowthisnews.com.

49. Quoted in Julia Preston, "How the Dreamers Learned to Play Politics," Politico, September 9, 2017. www.politico.com.

50. Quoted in Preston, "How the Dreamers Learned to Play Politics."

51. Quoted in America's Voice, "Dreamers and Allies Speak Out in Purple and Red States Across America," September 29, 2017. https://americasvoice.org.

American Immigration Council— www.americanimmigrationcouncil.org

The American Immigration Council is a nonprofit group that advocates for the rights of immigrants. It provides free legal services to detained immigrant mothers with children, sponsors lawsuits supporting immigrant rights, and provides lots of information and news on its website about all types of issues related to immigration law and immigrants, including the Dreamers.

America's Voice—https://americasvoice.org

America's Voice is an organization advocating for immigration reform. There is a lot of information about DACA, the Dreamers, immigration law, and current issues surrounding illegal immigration on its website.

Center for American Progress—www.americanprogress.org

The Center for American Progress is a liberal public policy research organization. It provides information about all types of public policy, including information related to the Dreamers, DACA, and proposed legislation and Dream Acts.

DreamACTivist—https://dreamactivist.org

DreamACTivist is a group of more than three hundred thousand Dreamer activists advocating for Dreamer rights. The group circulates petitions and organizes rallies and demonstrations, among other activities. It provides information and news related to the Dreamers on its website.

Dreamers Adrift—http://dreamersadrift.com

Dreamers Adrift is a media platform for Dreamers to make the public aware of their plight through the arts. The website offers videos, essays, stories, and poetry created by Dreamers and presenting their point of view. It also provides news about immigration-related issues.

Migration Policy Institute—www.migrationpolicy.org

The Migration Policy Institute is a nonpartisan think tank concerned with issues surrounding global immigration. It offers reports and news articles about DACA, the Dreamers, the American Dream and Promise Act, and government immigration policies.

National Immigration Forum—https://immigrationforum.org

The National Immigration Forum is an organization that advocates for the rights of immigrants and the value of immigration in the United States. It provides a wealth of information on its website about all kinds of issues related to immigrants and immigration, including information about the Dreamers, their impact on the economy, and the American Dream and Promise Act.

United We Dream—https://unitedwedream.org

United We Dream is the largest immigrant youth–led organization in the United States. It offers a wealth of information related to the Dreamers, including information about current and proposed immigration laws, updates on immigration raids, tips on defending against deportation, leadership training, and a blog. It has chapters throughout the country.

US Citizenship and Immigration Services—www.uscis.gov

The US Citizenship and Immigration Services provides information about DACA renewals, the DACA program, extending and renewing visas, becoming a US citizen, various versions of the Dream Acts, and other data related to immigration.

Books

A.R. Carser, *US Immigration Policy*. Minneapolis, MN: Abdo, 2018.

Stephen Currie, *Undocumented Immigrant Youth*. San Diego, CA: ReferencePoint, 2017.

Duchess Harris, *The Dreamers and DACA*. Minneapolis, MN: Abdo, 2019.

Cathleen Small, *Undocumented Immigrants*. Farmington Hills, MI: Lucent, 2018.

Internet Sources

Define American, "Stories," 2019. https://defineamerican.com.

Alan Gomez, "Who Are the DACA Dreamers and How Many Are Here?," *USA Today*, February 13, 2018. www.usatoday.com.

Kirk W. Johnson, "A DACA Recipient with an American Life Considers the Future," *New Yorker*, September 13, 2017. www.newyorker.com.

Parija Kavilanz, "America's Biggest Businesses Are Standing by Their Dreamer Employees," CNN, January 18, 2018. https://money.cnn.com.

LegalMatch, "Federal and State DREAM Acts." www.legalmatch.com.

New York Times, "American Dreamers." www.nytimes.com.

Cover: Mark Scott Spatny/Shutterstock

7: Shelia Fitzgerald/Shutterstock
11: Dan Howell/Shutterstock
15: Associated Press
20: Associated Press
24: Darren Eli/Polaris/Newscom
29: Krista Kennell/Shutterstock
31: Associated Press
35: Associated Press
37: kryzhov/Shutterstock
40: Monkey Business Images/iStock
46: Maury Aaseng
48: iStock
52: FatCamera/iStock
57: Associated Press
60: Douliery Olivier/Sipa USA/Newscom
63: Associated Press

Barbara Sheen is the author of 104 books for young people. She lives in New Mexico with her family. In her spare time she likes to swim, garden, walk, cook, and read.